Marvel's Thor

Based on the Screenplay by
Ashley Edward Miller & Zack Stentz and Don Payne

Story by J. Michael Straczynski and Mark Protosevich

Produced by Kevin Feige, p.g.a.
Directed by Kenneth Branagh

Level 3

Retold by Karen Holmes

Series Editors: Andy Hopkins and Jocelyn Potter

Pearson Education Limited

KAO Two

KAO Park, Harlow,

Essex, CM17 9NA, England

and Associated Companies throughout the world.

ISBN: 978-1-292-20599-1

This edition first published by Pearson Education Ltd 2018

3 5 7 9 10 8 6 4

Set in 9pt/14pt Xenois Slab Pro

SWTC/03

Published by Pearson Education Limited

For a complete list of the titles available in the Pearson English Readers series, visit
www.pearsonenglishreaders.com.
Alternatively, write to your local Pearson Education office or
to Pearson English Readers Marketing Department,
Pearson Education, KAO Two, KAO Park, Harlow, Essex, CM17 9NA

Contents

Who's Who?

Jane Foster

Jane Foster is a scientist who studies the stars. When she left college, she became interested in mysterious changes to the weather outside the small town of Puente Antiguo, New Mexico. Her assistant is college student Darcy Lewis.

Dr. Erik Selvig

Dr. Selvig is another scientist who studies the stars. He is a friend of Jane Foster's father. He works at a college in Virginia and taught Jane and Darcy there. He lives in the United States, but his family came from Norway.

S.H.I.E.L.D.

S.H.I.E.L.D. is a powerful U.S. agency. It was formed to protect the United States from attacks. Now, though, it also protects the world against attacks from space. Phil Coulson is one of S.H.I.E.L.D.'s most important agents.

Laufey and the Frost Giants

Laufey is the king of Jotunheim, one of the Nine Realms. In the past, he and Odin were enemies. Jotun warriors are called Frost Giants, and are very large. When they touch something, it turns to ice.

Odin

Odin is the king of Asgard, one of the Nine Realms. Brave and powerful, he wants to keep the peace between Asgard and other realms. When he fights, he uses his spear, Gungnir. He and his wife, Frigga, have two sons, Thor and Loki.

Thor

Thor is an Asgardian prince, the older son of Odin and Frigga. He was loved by them, and his brother Loki was his best friend. Now he is a brave, handsome, and popular young warrior. His hammer, Mjolnir, gives him great fighting power.

Loki

Loki, also an Asgardian prince, is the smart younger son of Odin and Frigga. Like Thor, he was taught to fight. Frigga also taught him to play tricks with other people's minds. Sometimes they see what he wants them to see, for example.

Lady Sif and the Warriors Three

When Lady Sif was a girl, nobody noticed her fighting skills. Thor believed in her, though. Now she and the Warriors Three—Fandral, Volstagg, and Hogun—are some of Asgard's greatest fighters. They are all close friends of Thor.

Heimdall

Heimdall is an Asgardian warrior. He can see and hear almost everything that happens in the Nine Realms. For that reason, he is Asgard's gatekeeper on the Bifrost, guarding Asgard against enemy attacks and other dangers.

Introduction

"Yes," his father said quietly. "I was stupid. You are not yet ready to be king. You did not listen to me! You must be punished, and you must learn to be a real king. You cannot do that in Asgard. I will take away your power and send you to another realm. Learn to put other people's needs before your own!"

Asgard, like Earth, is one of the Nine Realms of Yggdrasil. Yggdrasil—the "World Tree"—is an energy field that joins these realms together.

Odin, King of Asgard, is worried about his older son. Thor is brave, but he is also young, proud, and thoughtless. He does not follow his father's orders, and as a result he puts Asgard in great danger. Odin decides to take away Thor's special powers and send him to Earth. Maybe in another realm he will learn to be wiser.

When Thor arrives on Earth, he meets Jane Foster—a young scientist—and her friends. Can they help him to get back his power? Will Thor find his way home again? And will he win the love or hate of Odin's other son, his brother Loki?

Produced by Marvel Studios, *Thor* was first shown in 2011. Marvel is famous for its stories of powerful men and women from other worlds—*The Avengers, Guardians of the Galaxy 1 and 2, Captain America: Civil War …* Many of these stories are also Pearson English Readers.

The action in *Thor* takes place in three of the Nine Realms. Jane Foster and her friends live and work on Earth, in the United States. Thor's home is on Asgard. The third realm is the frozen land of Jotunheim. There is peace between the realms at the beginning of the story—but war is always possible.

Thor stars Chris Hemsworth as Thor, Natalie Portman as Jane Foster, and Anthony Hopkins as Odin. The movie, with its exciting story and great battles, was a big success around the world.

A Stranger Arrives

The air was dry and cold near the small town of Puente Antiguo, New Mexico. Darcy Lewis sat in the driver's seat of an old van full of expensive scientific equipment. She was a college student working with scientist Jane Foster. Another scientist, Dr. Erik Selvig, sat in the passenger seat.

In the back of the van, Jane opened the roof and climbed onto it. Selvig followed her, and they looked up into the darkness.

"So what exactly are we looking for?" Selvig asked. He was a friend of Jane's father and knew her well. "Why did you ask me to join you here in New Mexico?"

"I told you. Something strange is happening in the night sky and I need your help," Jane replied. "It's a little different each time. Once it was a pool of stars in a corner of the sky. But last week it was a rainbow—" A noise from her computer stopped her. "Wait for it!" she said excitedly.

Nothing happened. The sky above them stayed calm and black.

Darcy put her head out of the window and looked up at Jane. "Can I turn on the radio?" she asked. She sounded bored.

"No!" Jane replied angrily. She and Selvig climbed back inside the van. "I don't understand," she said. She opened a small book and looked at her notes. She always carried this notebook—inside it was her life's work.

"These changes have happened many times, always at night, Erik!" She checked her computer.

With her eyes on her computer, she didn't notice the strange clouds in the sky. All the colors of the rainbow, they came out of nowhere. But Darcy saw them.

"Jane?" she said over her shoulder. "You need to see this!"

"What?" Jane shouted.

The van started to shake. Jane lifted her head and looked through the front window. The stars seemed to be falling from the sky and grouping into a big cloud. The colored lights were stronger now.

The winds grew stronger, too. Then, at the center of the stars, a dark cloud began to turn faster and faster. The strange rainbow light grew brighter—and something fell to Earth from the sky. They couldn't see it clearly, but they heard it hit the ground.

"Closer! Go!" Jane shouted to Darcy.

Lightning hit the ground near them and the van shook on its wheels.

Darcy screamed. "That's enough!" she cried. "I'm done! I'm not dying to pass my college course!"

She tried to turn the van toward home, but Jane reached for the wheel.

Suddenly, the van's headlights lit up something in front of them and a large man walked out of the storm and into their path. His eyes were shut, so he couldn't see their van. Pulling at the wheel, Jane tried to drive around him. But she was too late and—*BAM!*—the van knocked him down.

The vehicle stopped. There was silence as Jane, Darcy, and Selvig looked at the body on the ground in front of them. Then they all jumped out.

Jane ran to the man. Was he alive? He was very handsome, with long fair hair. His face was beautiful; his chest and shoulders were wide and strong.

Is this guy famous? she thought. *This is going to get me in so much trouble.*

"Please don't be dead, big man," she said. Then she turned to Selvig and Darcy. "Where did he come from?" she asked.

Earlier that same day, Odin, King of Asgard, was in his palace. It was a very important day, but he was worried.

Inside the palace, thousands of Asgardians were waiting to welcome their new king—Odin's older son, Thor.

Odin was a strong king, but now he was tired. He had to go into the Odinsleep, the deep sleep that always made him strong again. Odinsleep only lasted for a few days—a week at the most—but during that time Odin lost his power. While Odin slept, Asgard needed another king.

Thor was a brave warrior, but he grew angry quickly and he loved to fight. That was why Odin was worried.

He sat at the front of the room, facing the crowd, with his wife, Frigga, and his younger son, Loki. Loki was Thor's opposite—quiet, always in the shadows. He watched and listened and he made his own plans. He wasn't known as a brave warrior, but he was very smart. He could play tricks with people's minds.

Nobody noticed Loki because he was the second son, the weaker son, the forgotten son. All eyes in Asgard followed Thor.

Suddenly, there was a lot of noise and Thor walked in. Proud and excited, he was dressed for battle and laughing loudly. He waved happily at his best friends, Lady Sif and the Warriors Three—Volstagg, Fandral, and Hogun.

As Thor lifted Mjolnir, his hammer, high above his head, he remembered his father's words from many years earlier: "My first-born son, Mjolnir's power is very great. You can use that power as a weapon. You can also use it as a tool to build a better world. Mjolnir will be a good friend to a wise king."

Lady Sif and Frigga smiled at Thor. Now he was waving at the crowd and shouting a battle cry. But Odin still looked worried. Was his first-born son *ready* to be king?

Thor arrived in front of his father, lowered his head, and waited. Silence fell over the crowd.

"A new day has come for a new king," Odin began. "Today, my son, you will become King of Asgard. Do you promise to guard the Nine Realms?"

"I promise," Thor replied.

Loki looked away angrily, but nobody noticed.

As Thor lifted Mjolnir, his hammer, high above his head, he remembered his father's words from many years earlier.

"Do you promise to keep the peace in the Nine Realms?" Odin asked.

"I promise."

"Do you promise to think of other people and not yourself? To think only of the good of the Nine Realms?"

"I promise!" Thor shouted, lifting Mjolnir high into the air.

"Then on this day—" Suddenly, Odin stopped. He felt strangely cold. The deep cold ran through his body. "Frost Giants!" he said quietly.

Frost Giants—Jotun warriors—came from the realm of Jotunheim. Many years earlier, Odin fought a long war with the Jotuns, on Earth. They wanted to turn Earth into a world of ice, but he stopped them and made peace with their king, Laufey. There was no reason now for the Jotuns to come to Asgard.

Suddenly, there was ice everywhere. Everything turned to ice when the Frost Giants touched it.

Odin hurried down to the underground room where the Destroyer guarded the Casket of Ancient Winters. Thor, Loki, the Warriors Three, and Lady Sif followed.

In the underground room, they saw two Frost Giants dead on the floor. Above them stood the Destroyer, a suit of armor three times bigger than a man that was filled with great power. It was the Destroyer's job to defend Asgard. Now, it held the casket in its hands.

"The Casket of Ancient Winters can bring never-ending winter. Laufey's power is in this box," Odin told the warriors. "I took it from him after our battle and brought it here. The casket is still safe because the Destroyer guards it at all times." He looked thoughtful. "But does Laufey really want to take the Nine Realms and turn them into frozen ice lands? Or is this the work of a few Jotuns? And how did they get into Asgard? Heimdall guards the Bifrost that joins Asgard to the Nine Realms. He sees everything. Nobody can come into Asgard unnoticed."

"If Jotuns have come into our realm," Thor shouted, "they must pay for their actions! This is an act of war!"

Odin shook his head sadly. He wanted peace for Asgard.

He turned to Lady Sif and the Warriors Three. "Leave us," he ordered. When he was alone with his sons, he asked Thor, "What action do you want to take?"

"I want to go to Jotunheim. I want to teach them a lesson."

"Many years ago, the Casket of Ancient Winters belonged to the Jotuns," Odin said.

"They will use it to destroy the Nine Realms!" Thor said.

"If this is the action of only a few Jotun warriors," Odin said, "we can make our realm safe. There is no need for a fight."

"As King of Asgard—" Thor began.

"But you're not king yet!" Odin shouted angrily. Loki watched with interest. "You think I am old and weak. But I am still your king. And *I* must guard Asgard. I am ordering you not to travel to Jotunheim. You will start a war!"

Thor's eyes shone angrily, but he didn't speak. He turned and walked away.

In the Land of the Frost Giants

Thor walked across the palace dining room to a long dinner table and threw it on its side. Food and drink, plates and glasses, crashed to the ground.

"We are going to Jotunheim," he shouted angrily to his friends.

"I agree with you," Loki said carefully, "that the Jotuns will come back again, maybe with thousands of warriors. But you cannot do anything about it. You must listen to Father."

But Thor wanted a battle. "My friends, we must do this. We must teach them a lesson," he told the warriors. He turned to Loki. "Will you come with me, little brother?"

"Of course," Loki said. "You cannot go alone."

The warriors looked worried.

"Thor, you must not break the laws of Asgard. You must listen to your father!" Lady Sif cried.

"My father fought a great war against the Jotuns and took their casket. Why did they come here now? We are only looking for answers. My friends, believe me. We must do this."

"Then I will be at your side," Volstagg said.

"I will be at your side, too," Fandral agreed.

"The Warriors Three fight together," Hogun said.

Lady Sif was worried but she agreed to fight, too.

While the others checked their weapons, Loki walked away quietly. When he joined them again, Hogun looked at him, a question in his eyes. Loki said nothing.

Excited now, they rode on horseback across the Rainbow Bridge. This bridge ran from the palace to Heimdall's guard post, the farthest place on Asgard. Heimdall could see everything that happened in the Nine Realms. At his post, there was a large, round, gold machine. When Heimdall placed his sword into the machine, it sent out a strong light—the Bifrost— through the sky. Asgardians could travel through the Bifrost to the other realms.

Before they reached the guard post, Thor, Loki and the warriors climbed down from their horses.

"We have to get past Heimdall," Thor said.

"That will not be easy," Volstagg agreed.

Heimdall answered only to the King of Asgard. He was, of course, waiting for them.

"Leave this to me," Loki said. "Heimdall—" he began.

Heimdall held up his hand. "Silence!" he said loudly. He looked at Loki. "Do you think you can use your tricks on me?" he asked.

Loki stepped back.

Thor moved closer. "Heimdall, can we pass?" he asked.

When Heimdall spoke, his words were slow and careful. "For hundreds of years I have guarded Asgard and kept it safe," he said. "In all that time, no enemy has come into the realm. How did that happen today? I want to know. Which traitor let the Jotuns in?"

"We will find out when we go to Jotunheim," Thor said. "Do not tell anyone where we are."

"Be careful," Heimdall said. "The Bifrost will stay closed if your return will hurt Asgard. You and your brother, and your friends, will not be able to leave Jotunheim."

That worried them all—except Thor.

"I have no plans to die today," he laughed.

Heimdall didn't smile. "Nobody *plans* to die," he said.

"Can't you leave the Bifrost open for us?" Volstagg asked nervously.

"No," Heimdall said. "Its energy is too powerful. If it stays open, it will destroy Jotunheim."

Thor looked at Lady Sif and the Warriors Three, and laughed again. "Let's go!" he said. "My friends, we are going to Jotunheim."

Heimdall lifted his large golden sword and pushed it down into the machine. The room filled with lightning, and then a bright light shot out into the dark sky toward Jotunheim. The Asgardians were pulled across by the great power of the Bifrost and arrived in seconds in the realm of ice.

Jotunheim was cold and dark and full of shadows.

"We shouldn't be here," Hogun said nervously.

Suddenly, a crowd of Frost Giants came out of the shadows. Their skin was a blue-gray color, their eyes were bright red, and they were very, very tall.

"What is your business here?" one of the Giants asked angrily.

Thor stepped toward them, but the Giants formed a tight circle around the Asgardians.

"I will speak only to your king," Thor said.

"Then speak," another voice said. A tall, thin Giant slowly walked toward him. He looked old, but his voice was proud. "I am Laufey," he said, "King of Jotunheim."

"I want answers!" Thor shouted. "How did your people get into Asgard?"

Laufey looked at him for a long time. Finally he said, "The house of Odin is full of traitors."

"Do not tell lies!" Thor cried.

"Why have you come here?" Laufey asked. "To make peace? No. You want a battle. You are a boy trying to be a man."

More Frost Giants moved closer to Thor and his friends.

Loki put his hand on his brother's arm. "There are too many of them," he said.

Thor looked around. Maybe his brother was right. Lady Sif and the Warriors Three were shaking their heads—they wanted to leave, too.

With one last look at Laufey, Thor turned to leave. And then one of the Frost Giants spoke.

"Run back to your home, little boy," it said quietly.

Thor smiled. Now he had a reason to fight. He turned and lifted his great hammer, Mjolnir. Slowly, Volstagg, Hogun, Fandral, and Lady Sif pulled out their weapons.

The Jotuns touched the cold water at their own feet. It froze their hands into dangerous ice weapons.

The battle started. Thor and his friends fought well, and Loki was next to them all the time. But then a strange thing happened to Loki. A Frost Giant attacked him and touched his arm. Loki looked down. His hand and arm were blue, and very, very cold.

Thor smiled. Now he had a reason to fight.

"These are the actions of a *boy*," Odin said. "We are *men*. We can stop this."

Surprised, the Frost Giant stopped fighting and looked at him. Loki killed the Giant immediately. Loki didn't understand the changes in his body—but he wanted to keep them secret.

Thor threw Mjolnir again and again and killed one Frost Giant after another. He lifted his hammer and lightning came down from the sky. He was laughing and enjoying the battle. But there were too many Jotuns. The Asgardians couldn't win.

Slowly, Laufey's warriors closed the circle around the Asgardians …

Back in Asgard, a guard ran to Odin. "Thor has taken his brother and his friends into Jotunheim," he said.

Angrily, Odin called for his horse. A few minutes later, the Bifrost took him to Jotunheim. When he arrived, the battle stopped.

"Father!" Thor shouted. "We will finish this together."

"Silence!" Odin shouted at his son.

Laufey spoke. "You look tired, Odin," he said.

Odin turned to him. "Laufey, end this," he ordered.

"Your boy started it," Laufey said.

"You're right. These are the actions of a *boy*," Odin said. "We are *men*. We can stop this."

Laufey shook his head. "No. Thor will get what he wants—war and death."

Odin saw that Laufey held an ice knife in his right hand.

Laufey lifted the knife—but Odin was ready. A hole opened in the sky and the Asgardians were pulled through the Bifrost, out of Jotunheim, to home.

In Asgard, Odin turned to his older son. "Are you sorry for your actions?" he asked angrily. "Can you see your mistakes?"

"The Jotuns must learn to fear me," Thor replied.

"Have you forgotten everything I taught you?" Odin asked. "Do you think only of yourself? A war with Jotunheim will kill thousands of innocent people."

"The Nine Realms are laughing at us!" Thor shouted.

"You are a proud, thoughtless boy," Odin cried.

"And you are a stupid old man!" Thor shouted back.

"Yes," his father said quietly. "I *was* stupid. You are not yet ready to be king. You did not listen to me! You must be punished, and you must learn to be a *real* king. You cannot do that in Asgard. I will take away your powers and send you to another realm. Learn to put other people's needs before your own!"

Odin pulled off pieces of Thor's armor. The Bifrost lit up and Odin pushed Thor into it. His son disappeared.

Odin put out his hand and the hammer, Mjolnir, flew into it.

"The next owner of this hammer will be strong and powerful. But he will also be wise," he said. "He will use the power of Mjolnir wisely."

Then Odin threw the hammer after Thor and it also disappeared.

The man on the ground stood up slowly. He looked down at his clothes, then up at the sky, and then at Jane.

"Are you O.K.?" Jane asked.

The man looked around. "Hammer?" he said finally. Then, more loudly, he called, "Hammer!"

Jane didn't know what to say. Then, out of the corner of her eye, she saw strange shapes in the sand. They were in the place where the strange man landed. She stopped thinking about him.

"We need to record these shapes quickly, before anything changes," she said, excited. She reached for her notebook.

Selvig spoke. "Jane, we need to take this man to a hospital."

Jane continued writing notes. "He's O.K."

The man pointed at the sky. "Father! Heimdall!" he screamed. "I know you can hear me! Open the Bifrost!"

Jane looked at him. "Maybe he's *not* O.K.," she said slowly. "You and Darcy take him to the hospital. I'll stay here."

She turned back to her notebook.

The man went to Darcy. "You!" he shouted. "What realm is this?"

"Uh … New Mexico," Darcy said. This man was very handsome—but he also seemed crazy, and very angry.

When he moved closer, she stepped back. She reached into her pocket and pulled out her Taser.

"Do you think you can attack Thor with that—"

Thor didn't finish his sentence. Darcy shot at him with the Taser and he fell to the ground.

Jane looked up from her notebook. The man wasn't moving. "O.K.," she said. "We'll *all* go to the hospital."

They drove away. Behind them a large, heavy object fell from the sky and landed on the ground.

Puente Antiguo hospital wasn't busy. A young nurse sat behind the desk. "Name?" she asked.

"He says it's Thor," Jane answered.

"And how do you know him?"

"I've never met him before," Jane said.

"Until she hit him with the van," Darcy added.

Jane looked angrily at her assistant.

"I need a name and a telephone number," the nurse said.

Selvig gave her his card. "You can reach us here," he said.

Jane watched some other nurses take Thor away.

We've done what we can for him, she thought. *So why don't I want to leave him?*

Back in her office, Jane and Selvig printed the pictures of the sky from her computer.

"These clouds seem to join different stars," Jane explained, pointing at the rainbow-colored clouds.

Suddenly Darcy said, "Look at this."

She held up a picture of a cloud of stars. There, in the middle, was Thor, falling from the sky! They all looked at the picture in surprise.

"I must go back to the hospital," Jane said finally. "I need to talk to Thor. Now!"

But when they arrived, his room was empty. The bed was in pieces on the floor.

"So, now what?" Darcy asked, when they were in the parking lot again.

"We find him," Jane answered. "We must talk to him."

She got into the driver's seat, and started the van. *BAM!*

"You've hit something—again," Darcy said.

It was Thor! And he was lying on the ground—again.

Jane jumped out of the van. "I'm so sorry!" she shouted.

Thor didn't say anything for a minute. Then slowly, he opened his eyes and looked up at the sun. "Blue sky, one sun," he said softly. "Oh, no! This is Earth, isn't it?"

Loki Learns a Secret

Jane, Darcy, and Selvig took Thor to their office. Jane found an old boyfriend's clothes for him and he put on the jeans and a T-shirt. He started to walk around the office, looking at their equipment.

Darcy watched him. "He's a crazy homeless person—but he's very handsome," she said to Jane.

Jane was thinking the same thing. She couldn't help liking this strange, big man.

Thor stopped in front of the pictures from the storm.

"What were you doing there?" Jane asked.

Thor looked closer. "Coming down the Bifrost," he said.

Excited, Jane wrote the words in her notebook. What was the Bifrost? Did it come from the sky? To Thor, it was clearly nothing special.

"I feel weak," Thor said suddenly. "I need food."

Soon he, Jane, Selvig, and Darcy were sitting in a café in town. There was enough food on the table for four people and Thor ate it all.

He took a large drink of coffee. "This drink," he said. "I like it." He threw the cup on the floor, and it broke. "Bring me another one!" he shouted.

Jane looked at the waitress. "Sorry," she said. "It was an accident." She turned to Thor. "Why did you do that?" she asked angrily.

"The drink was delicious," Thor said. "I want another."

"Then ask nicely," she said.

"I did!" Thor replied.

Two men came into the café and sat down.

"You missed all the fun outside town," one of them said loudly to the waitress, after they ordered.

"A large object crashed into the ground last night," the other man added. He sounded very excited.

Selvig walked across the room to them. "What was it?" he asked.

"I don't know, but it's very heavy," the first man answered. "It's like a big hammer and nobody can lift it out of the ground. Hundreds of men have tried. We were enjoying ourselves until the soldiers arrived."

Thor jumped to his feet. "Where is it?" he shouted.

"Uh—uh—about eighty kilometers west of here," the man said nervously.

"But don't go there," his friend said. "There are a lot of soldiers and government agents guarding it!"

Thor smiled, and then he walked out of the restaurant into the middle of the road. Cars had to stop or drive around him.

Jane ran after him. "Where are you going?" she asked.

"To get something that belongs to me," Thor said.

"But there are guards around it," Jane replied. "What will you do? Walk in and take it?"

"Yes." Thor looked at her. "Listen, I will tell you everything if you take me there."

"Everything?" Jane asked.

"You can have all the answers—when I get Mjolnir."

"Mjolnir?" Jane repeated. "What's Mjolnir?"

Selvig pulled Jane away from Thor.

"Please don't listen to him," he told her. "He's crazy! These words—'Thor,' 'Mjolnir'—I've heard them before in Scandinavian children's stories! He's crazy, and maybe dangerous!"

Jane looked at the two men.

"I'm sorry," she said to Thor finally. "I can't drive you."

"I understand," Thor said. "So we must say goodbye."

He looked into her eyes and kissed her hand.

Jane smiled. Suddenly, she felt very shy. "Thank you," she said.

"Jane Foster, Erik Selvig, Darcy," Thor said. "Goodbye." Then he walked away.

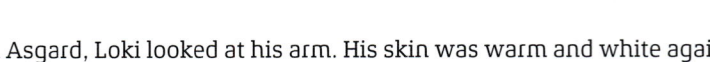

In Asgard, Loki looked at his arm. His skin was warm and white again. *What happened to me in Jotunheim?* he asked himself.

"Why didn't we stop Thor going to Jotunheim?" Volstagg asked sadly.

"How could we?" Lady Sif replied.

"How did Odin know that we were *in* Jotunheim?" Volstagg asked.

Loki looked at him. "I told one of his guards."

"*You* told a guard?" Volstagg shouted angrily.

"I saved our lives!" Loki said. "And Thor's."

"Loki," Lady Sif said, "only you can help Thor now. Go to Odin. Ask him to change his mind and bring Thor back to Asgard."

"Then what will happen?" Loki asked. "I love Thor, but he is proud and dangerous. You saw him today. He wants war. Do *you* think he's ready to be Asgard's king?"

Lady Sif and the Warriors Three didn't answer, and Loki left the room.

"Loki often talks about his love for Asgard. But his feelings for Thor are not so simple," Lady Sif said. "*He* would like to be the older brother—and to be king!"

"That's true, but he did save our lives," Volstagg said.

Hogun spoke. "Laufey talked about a traitor inside Asgard. Is Loki the traitor? Did *he* bring the Jotuns here?"

"No!" Volstagg said. "Loki plays tricks with people's minds, but he is not a traitor!"

Lady Sif spoke slowly. "Someone tricked Heimdall and got past him. That person let the Jotuns into Asgard. We must tell Odin. Asgard is in danger if Loki *is* working with the Jotuns."

"You were an innocent child," Odin said.

Loki went down to the underground room. He knew that Sif and the warriors were talking about him. They were Thor's friends, not his.

He picked up the Casket of Ancient Winters with both hands. His hands turned blue again and he felt cold deep inside his body.

"Stop!" a voice shouted from the end of the room.

Loki turned and saw his father. Odin looked old and tired.

"What is happening to me?" Loki asked him.

"Put down the casket," Odin said.

When Loki put down the casket, his body felt warm again. The blue color disappeared.

"What am I?" he asked.

"You are my son," Odin answered.

But Loki suddenly understood. "This casket wasn't the only thing that you took from Jotunheim on the last day of the war ..." he said slowly.

"No," Odin agreed. "After the battle, I found a baby alone in a church. He was left there to die. He was Laufey's son." Odin was silent for a minute, and then he said, "That was you."

"Laufey's son ..." Loki repeated. "Why? You were at war. Why did you take me?"

"You were an innocent child," Odin said.

But Loki knew there was more. "You took me for a reason," he said angrily. "What was it? Tell me!"

"I wanted to join Jotunheim and Asgard. I wanted to bring peace to

"You can talk to me—your king."

both realms one day, through you," Odin said.

Loki felt angry and hurt. "So I am a stolen child, here only for that one reason. Now I understand why Thor is your favorite son," he said. "I am a Jotun. I can never be King of Asgard!"

"You are my son! I didn't tell you because I wanted to protect you."

Odin's body began to shake. He felt very weak and he held out his hand to Loki. Then he fell to the ground and his eyes closed.

There were tears in Loki's eyes. He touched his father's hand, then shouted, "Guards! Please, help!"

An hour later, Lady Sif and the Warriors Three went to see the king. With their heads down, they walked toward his great chair.

"Odin," Sif said, "we must speak with you. It is very important."

Then she stopped. In front of them sat Loki. In his right hand he held Odin's spear, Gungnir.

"What is this?" Volstagg asked.

"My friends," Loki said, "I am now King of Asgard."

"Where is Odin?" Fandral asked.

"Father has fallen into the Odinsleep," Loki replied. He sounded very sad. "It is different this time. My mother is afraid that he will not wake up again."

"Can we speak to her?" Lady Sif asked.

Loki shook his head. "She will not leave my father's bedside," he said. He stood up. "You can talk to me—your king."

Lady Sif and the Warriors Three went slowly down on their knees.

"My king, please end Thor's punishment and bring him back," Lady Sif said.

"My father sent Thor away. It was his last order and I cannot change it," Loki said. "There is a strong possibility of war with Jotunheim. People need to know who their king is. They don't want more change—they need to feel safe."

The warriors were angry, but they couldn't disagree with him.

"Of course," Fandral said.

They stood up, and slowly left the room. They didn't speak again until they were far away from Loki.

The Fight for Mjolnir

When Jane Foster and her friends returned to her office, it was full of government agents. In the parking lot, men were pulling her van to pieces. More agents came out of the office with computers, boxes, and papers in their arms.

Jane ran forward. "What's happening here?" she shouted.

One of the men stepped toward her and held out his hand.

"Ms. Foster," he said. "I'm Agent Coulson, from S.H.I.E.L.D. There's a serious problem and our country's not safe. We need your equipment and your papers."

"You can't take them!" Jane said angrily. "This is important work! We're making new, exciting discoveries."

She held up her notebook.

Coulson picked up the box at his feet and took the notebook from Jane's hand.

"We're the good guys," he said. "I'm sorry, Ms. Foster. Thank you for your help."

He and the other agents left the empty office and drove away.

"Years of work, gone," Jane said sadly. "They took everything. Who are these people?"

"I've heard of S.H.I.E.L.D.," Selvig said. "It's a very powerful government agency. In the beginning, it protected the U.S. Now, I think, it protects the world. I knew a scientist who was doing some secret work. One day S.H.I.E.L.D. arrived ... Nobody saw her again—ever. You can't fight S.H.I.E.L.D."

"I'm going to get all my work back," Jane said.

She looked out the window. Across the street, she saw Thor. He was still in town—and he was walking into a pet store.

Jane ran down the street and followed him into the store.

"I need a horse," Thor was saying loudly.

"We don't have any horses," the assistant replied. "We sell dogs and cats ..."

"Give me a big one of those," Thor ordered. "One that I can ride."

"I'll drive you," Jane said quickly.

A few minutes later, she and Thor were in the van. The sun was going down and there were storm clouds in the evening sky.

"I've never broken into a place before," Jane said. "Have you?"

"Many times," Thor laughed. He looked at her thoughtfully. "Do you think I am strange?" he asked.

"Well ... a little."

"Good strange or bad strange?"

"I'm not sure," Jane replied. "But who are you really?"

"You will see soon," Thor said. He smiled at her. "The colored lights that you saw in the sky? They are a bridge—a bridge between different realms."

Jane stopped the van on a small hill. She and Thor looked down. The strange, heavy object from the sky was on the ground below them. There were bright lights around it and a wall with high metal gates to keep people out. And there were guards everywhere, all with guns.

"They've already put up offices around it!" Jane said in surprise.

There were small buildings made of metal and plastic sheets. On the side of one of them, Jane saw the word *S.H.I.E.L.D.* in big white letters.

Thor put his jacket around her shoulders. "You will need this," he said.

"Why?" Jane asked.

There was the sound of thunder and rain began to fall.

He smiled again and pulled, but Mjolnir didn't move.

"Stay here," Thor said. "I will get Mjolnir, then I will find your notes and equipment. O.K.?"

"No!" Jane said. "Look down there! Look at all the guards! You can't walk in, and walk out!"

"No," Thor agreed. "I am going to fly out."

He walked away. Lightning lit up the sky and the storm began.

Thor started to make a hole in the ground under one of the metal gates. In a few minutes, he was inside. Because of the lightning, some guards saw him and ran toward him. Thor fought the first guards and easily knocked them down.

As he ran toward the nearest building, he met another soldier. Thor knocked him down, too. More soldiers came to help their friend. Thor fought them all.

There were cameras everywhere around Mjolnir. In the main office, Agent Coulson watched Thor on a computer. Worried, he called one of his men.

"Take a gun. Watch the big guy and wait for my orders," he said.

The gunman went out into the rain and climbed a high building. He could see Thor clearly from the roof. He pointed his weapon.

"Shall I shoot him?" he asked Coulson over his radio.

"Not yet," Coulson said. "Let's see what happens next."

Thor ran toward Mjolnir. He was almost there when a very big, tall soldier stepped around the corner. He attacked Thor and they started to fight.

"You're big," Thor said with a smile. "But I've fought bigger."

They fought hard for a long time. The soldier was strong, but finally Thor knocked him down. The man didn't move again.

Up on the roof, the gunman smiled. "I'm starting to like this guy," he said over his radio to Coulson. "Do you really want me to shoot him?"

"Wait," Coulson said again.

Thor ran around a corner and smiled. There was Mjolnir! Now he could get back his power. Bright blue light traveled from the hammer toward Thor and up into the sky.

Thor reached down and touched the ancient war hammer. He smiled again and pulled, but Mjolnir didn't move. What was wrong? Why didn't he have any power over the hammer? Then he remembered his father's words: "The next owner of this hammer will be strong and powerful. But he will also be wise."

Thor looked up at the stormy sky. "*Noooo!*" he shouted.

He fell to his knees, and tears and rain ran down his face.

Thor didn't fight when the guards took him away.

In the main office, Coulson called the gunman on his radio. "You can come down now."

Up in Asgard, Heimdall looked down to Earth and watched Thor.

Jane watched him, too, from up on the hill. After a long time, she ran to the van and drove back to the office. She told her friends about Thor and Mjolnir.

"He's a criminal," Selvig said. "He's in prison now. What's the problem?"

"I can't leave him there!" Jane shouted.

Darcy showed her a children's picture book. "Look!" she said.

There was a picture of a hammer and it had a name: Mjolnir.

Jane took the book from Darcy. "Where did you find this?"

Selvig answered, "We were working in the library. We found it there. I told you! Thor is telling you silly stories. We're *scientists*, Jane!"

"Maybe there really *is* a kind of bridge of light that travels through the sky. Maybe people from other worlds crossed it thousands of years ago," Jane said. "That's where these stories came from. Thor and his hammer were here on Earth before! Maybe it *is* science but we don't understand it yet."

Selvig was silent for a minute while he thought about this. Finally, he spoke. "I don't understand any of this, Jane," he said. "But I'll help you. We'll get Thor out of there."

"Thank you, Erik," she said.

Selvig made a phone call. He had an escape plan for Thor.

Thor sat on a chair. There were small cuts on his face but the pain was inside him. Agent Coulson was trying without success to question him.

"In a fight, my men couldn't win against you. That hurts me. Who are you? Are you a soldier?" Coulson asked. "Where did you learn to fight? We *will* find out."

Thor didn't answer any of the agent's questions. Finally, Coulson left the room and Thor lowered his head.

When he looked up, Loki was standing in front of him. He was wearing a suit and tie and a long, black coat. He looked like a U.S. government agent.

"Loki? What are you doing here?" Thor said in surprise. Then he noticed that his brother was looking very serious. "What has happened?"

"I needed to see you," Loki said. "Father is dead. Your actions ... the possibility of a new war with the Jotuns—it was too much for him ..."

"What?" There were tears in Thor's eyes. Loki's plan was working. "My actions and words killed my father?"

"I know that you loved him." Loki said. "I tried to tell Father—but he did not listen." He waited, and then he said, "I am King of Asgard now."

First, the news of his father, and now this. Thor tried to understand.

"Can I come home?" he asked hopefully.

"Mother does not want you to return," Loki said sadly. "And the peace agreement with Jotunheim will end if you do not stay here." He turned away from Thor. "Goodbye, brother. I am very sorry."

"No," Thor said. "*I* am sorry. Loki ... thank you for coming here."

Loki left the room and went straight to Mjolnir. He tried to lift it, but it didn't move.

Agent Coulson returned to Thor's room. "You have a visitor," he said. Behind him was Dr. Selvig.

"Donny, Donny, there you are!" Selvig said. He turned to Coulson. "Yes, this is Dr. Donald Blake. He's a scientist who works with me. He's usually a wonderful man. But when you took our work, he went crazy. He wanted to get it back. Donny," he said to Thor, "it's going to be O.K. I'm taking you home."

Thor was too unhappy to make sense of Selvig's words. But on the way out of the building, he saw Jane's notebook on a table and picked it up.

Agent Coulson looked up from his computer and a picture of the real Dr. Donald Blake, and watched the two men leave.

"Follow them," he said to one of his agents.

When they were in the van, Selvig turned to Thor. "I'm only helping you because of Jane. Her father and I were teachers together."

"I will never hurt her," Thor said.

"Good." Selvig started the van. "But I've seen the way that she looks at you. I want you to leave town. Stay away from her."

Loki's Plan

Loki left his brother, but he didn't return to Asgard. He traveled to the icy realm of Jotunheim. This was the realm of his enemies—but it was also, he now knew, his true home.

Frost Giants came out of the darkness with Laufey at their head. Laufey's red eyes burned out of the darkness. Loki stepped toward him.

"Kill him," Laufey ordered the Frost Giants.

"After all that I have done for you?" Loki said calmly.

Laufey looked at him closely. "So *you* are the traitor who let us into Asgard," he said.

Loki smiled. "That was fun. It destroyed my brother's big day."

But Laufey was angry. "Some of my soldiers are dead and I still do not have the Casket of the Ancient Winters."

He reached out and attacked Loki. Loki didn't fight back. His skin turned blue and cold when Laufey touched him.

"You don't know who I am," Loki said. He smiled. "Hello, Father."

"Ah," Laufey said in surprise. "So Odin took you—but he did not kill you. He's a weak man—and you are weak, too."

"I am not weak now. I am King of Asgard, until Odin wakes up," Loki said. "I want to suggest something. I will hide you and your Frost Giants in Odin's palace. I will take you into Odin's bedroom, and you can kill him. Then I will be King of Asgard forever, and you can have the casket. There will be peace between our two realms. Peace that *I* have made, not Odin or Thor."

Laufey thought about it. Then he smiled at Loki. "This is a great day for Jotunheim. Asgard will finally be ours."

"No. Asgard is *mine*," Loki said. "The *other* parts of the Nine Realms will be yours."

For a minute, Laufey didn't speak. Then he said, "I accept."

When Loki returned to Asgard, he met Heimdall at his guard post at the end of the Rainbow Bridge.

Heimdall looked closely at him. "You have come from Jotunheim, but I could not see you there. I could not hear your words," he said. "You were hidden from me. When the Jotuns came into Asgard, they were also hidden from me."

He knows that I let the Jotuns into Asgard, Loki thought. *But I do not want to fight with him. He is too strong.*

"Maybe you are getting old," he said. "You have great power, Heimdall. Did Odin ever fear you?"

"No," Heimdall said. "He was my king. I promised to do all that he asked."

"And now *I* am your king," Loki said. "You work for *me*."

For a long time, Heimdall didn't reply. Then he said, "Yes."

"Good," Loki said. "Close the Bifrost. Don't open it for anyone!"

He walked away, but Heimdall was watching him.

Thor and Selvig went back to Jane's office. Jane noticed immediately that there was something different about Thor. He was quieter and sadder.

Thor looked up at the night sky. Finally, he spoke. His voice was deep and sad.

"Can we go outside?" Jane asked him. She wanted to talk to him alone. They left the office and went up to the roof.

"I come up here sometimes when I can't sleep," she said. "Or when Darcy's making me crazy."

Thor looked up at the night sky. Finally, he spoke. His voice was deep and sad. He told her about Odin.

"My father thought that I was young and thoughtless. I loved fighting too much. I did not think about other people. He sent me away from my home and family in Asgard, and I miss them. And my father is dead. But you have been very kind to me. I am grateful for your help."

"Well, I drove into you twice!" Jane said.

Thor took her notebook out of his pocket and held it out to her.

"This is all that I found. I'm sorry."

"Oh, I don't believe it! This is wonderful. Now I can continue with my work. I won't have to start again. Thank you so much," Jane said softly. Then she looked away from him.

"What's wrong?" Thor asked.

"S.H.I.E.L.D.," she answered. "I don't know who or what they really are. But they don't want anyone to know about my work."

"You must finish it. Never give up. Your ideas are correct."

He took her notebook and opened it. He smiled, and then he drew a picture. Slowly he started to explain.

"This is Yggdrasil, the World Tree—an energy field. Everything comes from this. The tree reaches out to the Nine Realms. Your world—Midgard, or Earth—is one of the Nine Realms. My home, Asgard, is another realm. We are all joined together by the World Tree."

He looked at Jane. She was listening carefully.

She is very beautiful, Thor thought.

In Asgard, Lady Sif and the Warriors Three were worried about the future of their realm—and also about Thor.

"We must go to Midgard," Hogun said. "We must find Thor."

"Loki will kill us," Fandral said.

"We are going to die!" Volstagg agreed.

The warriors were silent. It was true. Loki was their enemy now.

"Thor is our friend. We cannot leave him there," Lady Sif said quietly.

Suddenly, a guard came into the room. "Heimdall wants to see you," he said.

"Oh, no!" Volstagg said. "Heimdall sees everything. He's listening to us! He will be very angry."

They found Heimdall at the end of the Rainbow Bridge. He looked at them for a long time and then he spoke.

"Loki has given orders, but you have decided not to follow them. You plan to bring Thor back?"

Lady Sif looked at Heimdall. "Yes," she said, "but—"

"Good," Heimdall said.

"So, you will help us?" Volstagg asked.

"Loki is my king. I cannot open the Bifrost for you," Heimdall said. Then he left them.

"Now what can we do?" Volstagg asked.

Lady Sif noticed something. "Look!"

Heimdall's sword was in the machine that opened the Bifrost. Now *they* could open it.

From the palace roof, Loki watched the Bifrost light up between Asgard and Earth.

Lady Sif and the other warriors were gone when Heimdall returned. Suddenly, Loki arrived at the guard post and stopped a few meters in front of Heimdall. He carried Odin's spear, Gungnir.

"Tell me, Loki," Heimdall said. "How did you let the Jotuns into Asgard?"

"You think that the Bifrost is the only way in and out of Asgard?" Loki asked. "No—there are secret paths between the Nine Realms. But I do not need them now. You are a traitor! You watched while Lady Sif and the Warriors Three went through the Bifrost!" he said angrily. "You are not now the guard of the bridge. And you are not, now, an Asgardian!"

"Then I do not have to listen to you."

Heimdall lifted his sword and tried to cut Loki, but Loki moved faster. He pointed Gungnir at Heimdall, and ice poured from it. Loki's skin turned blue and his eyes turned the red color of his true father.

The ice covered Heimdall's body and then his face. He couldn't move. He stood, frozen, outside his guard post at the end of the Rainbow Bridge.

Slowly the blue color left Loki's skin and his eyes turned their usual color again. He walked away and went down to the underground room, to the Casket of Ancient Winters.

He opened the gate that held back the Destroyer. The Destroyer stepped forward.

"My brother must not return to Asgard," Loki said. "Stop him. Destroy him."

The ice covered Heimdall's body and then his face. He couldn't move. He stood, frozen, outside his guard post at the end of the Rainbow Bridge.

Agent Coulson was in his office near Puente Antiguo with other S.H.I.E.L.D. agents when they noticed big changes in the sky.

"What's that?' Coulson asked.

"I don't know, sir," a scientist replied. "A lot of energy appeared and then disappeared twenty-five kilometers north-west of here."

"Let's go and take a look," Coulson said. He went out of the office with his men and they got into their cars.

Four Friends—and
a Dangerous Enemy

Next day, Jane tried to explain Thor's stories of the Nine Realms of Yggdrasil and the Bifrost to Selvig and Darcy. Thor was making breakfast at the other end of the room.

"They're interesting ideas, Jane," Selvig said. "But no scientist will believe you."

Before Jane replied, there was a knock on the door. They all looked up and saw four people standing outside: three big, dangerous-looking men, and a woman. She looked even more dangerous than the men. They were all in armor and were carrying strange, old weapons.

"My friends!" Thor shouted happily, running to them.

"I don't believe it!" Selvig said. Who were these people?

Thor put his arm around Volstagg. "My friends," he said, "I am very pleased to see you, but it is not safe for you here."

"We are here to take you home," Fandral said.

"You know that I cannot go home," Thor said. "My father is dead because of my actions. I must stay here on Earth."

The warriors looked surprised.

"Thor," Lady Sif said, "your father is not dead. He is deep in the Odinsleep—and this time he was not prepared for it—but he is not dead."

Lightning lit up the sky, and there was a crash of thunder. But it was not a storm—it was the Bifrost. Someone—or something—was following the four warriors from Asgard to Earth.

A great cloud formed in the sky and a very large piece of metal in the shape of a man fell to Earth. It was the Destroyer, and now it was just outside Puente Antiguo.

Coulson and the other S.H.I.E.L.D. agents arrived in their cars.

Coulson got out. "Who are you?" he shouted.

The Destroyer stood in front of them, and his body filled with fire. He shot the fire from his eyes toward the agents' cars and destroyed them. Coulson and his agents ran for their lives. Even S.H.I.E.L.D. couldn't fight this—thing!

As the Destroyer walked into the town, the wind grew stronger. Most people ran into their houses, but Jane, her friends, Thor, and the warriors went into the street.

"What *is* that thing? Why is it here?" Jane asked.

"I do not know why the Destroyer is here," Thor said. "Maybe Father is teaching me another lesson. Jane, you must leave now."

"No!" She shook her head. "What are you going to do?" she asked.

Volstagg stepped forward. "He's going to fight with us, of course!"

Thor turned to his friends. "Not today," he said sadly. "I am just a man. I do not have my Asgardian powers here. *You* must stop the Destroyer. I will help people leave this town, but I will need some time."

"You will *have* time!" Volstagg cried.

"I'm staying if you're staying," Jane said to Thor.

Lady Sif and the Warriors Three ran toward the Destroyer.

Selvig went into the café. It was full of young mothers and their children. "Everybody out!" he shouted. "Use the back door."

The customers hurried outside and Thor lifted them into the backs of trucks.

Jane started shouting at other people on the sidewalks: "Leave town! Go as far away as you can."

Soon the streets were empty.

The Destroyer continued walking slowly down the main street, shooting fire everywhere. Houses, stores, and cars burned.

The four warriors walked toward it. Volstagg was laughing. He enjoyed a good battle.

Jane, Thor, Selvig, and Darcy went back to the office. They could hear the sounds of fighting. Then they heard a shout—a war cry.

Worried, Thor ran back outside. Jane and the others followed. Puente Antiguo's streets were destroyed. In front of them, the warriors were fighting hard.

Suddenly, Volstagg ran toward Fandral. Fandral went down on his knees and joined his hands together. Volstagg stepped up onto them, and Fandral threw him at the Destroyer. Volstagg was very big; no enemy could stand against him.

But the Destroyer did. It lifted its hand and hit Volstagg. The big man flew high into the air and then fell down on top of a car. The Destroyer walked toward him. The fire in its eyes was burning brightly.

Then Lady Sif jumped from the roof of the nearest building onto the Destroyer's back. Her spear was in her hand and she pushed it into the back of the Destroyer's neck. It cut through the metal man and went down into the ground. The Destroyer stopped moving and fell. The fire

in its eyes finally went out.

The warriors laughed. "You have destroyed the Destroyer!" Volstagg shouted to Lady Sif.

But they quickly stopped laughing when the Destroyer moved again. Its head turned, and its hands opened and closed. The fire inside it started to burn. Then it turned its great head toward Lady Sif. She jumped away as it shot fire at her.

The Destroyer stood up slowly. It sent its fire down the street. Lady Sif was thrown to the ground, and Volstagg and Hogun fell back through the café window.

"Go! Now! Run!" Thor told Jane.

Jane, Darcy, and Selvig ran away from the Destroyer. Thor ran, too—toward Lady Sif. She was still on the ground.

The Destroyer turned to her again.

"Sif," Thor shouted, "run! You cannot do any more."

"No," she said. "I will die a warrior's death. People will tell stories about this day."

"Live, and *you* can tell those stories," Thor said. "Volstagg is hurt. Go and help him. Return to Asgard and stop Loki."

"What will *you* do?" Lady Sif asked.

"Don't worry, my friends." Thor looked at the Destroyer. "I have a plan."

Lady Sif and the Warriors Three ran down the sidewalk, pulling Jane, Darcy, and Selvig with them. Thor walked slowly toward the Destroyer.

Lady Sif's spear was in her hand and she pushed it into the back of the Destroyer's neck.

Jane stopped running and turned. "What's he doing?" she asked her friends.

"Brother," Thor said. He knew that, up in Asgard, Loki was listening. "I am sorry you are angry. I am truly sorry if I hurt you in the past. But these people are innocent. It will not help you if you kill them."

Thor stopped and looked at the Destroyer. It wasn't moving, but there were only three meters between them and fire still burned brightly inside its eyes.

"So kill *me*. Take my life and stop this battle," Thor told his brother.

He waited. The fire in the Destroyer's eyes stopped burning. Slowly it stepped back, and then it walked away.

A tear ran down Thor's face. Loki and he were brothers. Loki was listening to him and now he, Thor, was safe.

But suddenly the Destroyer stopped, turned around, and hit Thor hard across the face. Thor flew through the air and crashed into a street more than a block away.

"No!" Jane shouted.

She ran to him, with Thor's friends close behind her.

The Destroyer walked away, out of town.

Thor lay on the ground. Jane sat next to him and touched his face. His eyes opened slowly, but he was very badly hurt.

"It is finished," he said quietly.

"No. It's *not* finished," she replied.

"I mean, you are safe," Thor said. "It is finished."

"No," Jane said. "*We're* safe." She started to cry. There were tears on her friends' faces, too.

Thor closed his eyes.

The Return to Asgard

Outside the town, the S.H.I.E.L.D. scientists were still studying the hammer.

"This is strange," one of the scientists said. "Energy is pouring into the hammer from the sky. I don't understand—" He didn't finish his sentence.

Mjolnir started to move. It broke free of the ground, and flew high into the sky, toward Puente Antiguo.

In the town, Selvig looked up into the sky. Was that thunder? Then he saw a big metal hammer coming through the clouds. It was falling toward Jane and Thor at great speed. He ran to them.

"Jane!" Selvig shouted, pulling her away from Thor.

"No! No! No!" Jane cried, not wanting to leave Thor's side.

Just before the hammer hit him, Thor opened his eyes. He lifted his hand and caught it. Lightning filled the sky. Then his jeans and T-shirt disappeared and shining armor took their place. In his right hand he held Mjolnir.

As he sat up, he remembered his father's words: "The next owner of this hammer will be strong and powerful. But he will also be wise. He will use the power of Mjolnir wisely."

"Oh, my God!" Jane said quietly, unable to take her eyes off Thor. He smiled at her.

Just outside Puente Antiguo, the Destroyer turned. It walked back into the town and down the main street toward Thor.

With a battle cry, Thor threw Mjolnir at the Destroyer. Then Mjolnir returned to Thor's hand and lifted him into the air. A storm grew around him, and lifted the Destroyer off the ground, too.

High above the town, the Destroyer attacked Thor again and again, and shot fire at him. And every time, Thor stopped the fire with Mjolnir.

Mjolnir's power pushed the Destroyer's fire back inside its body. The fire grew inside the Destroyer until it destroyed the great metal suit. Finally, the suit broke into pieces and fell to Earth.

Thor landed on the ground a few seconds later. He was even more handsome in his armor.

"Is this how you always look?" Jane asked.

"Most of the time," Thor said.

"It's a good look," she said, and smiled.

Thor turned to Lady Sif and the Warriors Three. "We must return to Asgard," he said. "I need to talk to my brother."

Just then, a big black car arrived and some S.H.I.E.L.D. agents got out. One of them was Agent Coulson. He looked at Thor.

"Donald, I don't think you've been completely honest with me," he said.

"You and I fight for the same reason: to protect this world," Thor said. "From this day, I will be your friend. But you must return the work that you took from Jane Foster."

"*Stole* from me," Jane said.

"We didn't *steal* it," Agent Coulson said. "We *borrowed* it. Of course you can have your equipment back. You'll need it for your work. Your discoveries are going to be very important."

Thor couldn't wait. It was time to return to his home and his father.

"Do you want to see the Bifrost?" he asked Jane.

"Uh … yes," she said.

Thor put his arm around her waist and held her close. He lifted

Heimdall could hear Thor's voice. Asgard needed him, but he was still covered in ice. He was still Loki's prisoner!

Mjolnir and he and Jane flew into the sky together. A few minutes later, they stood at the place outside Puente Antiguo where Thor and Mjolnir landed a day earlier.

Thor looked up into the sky and called, "Heimdall, open the Bifrost."

Nothing happened. He waited, and then shouted again. "Heimdall!"

Just then, Jane's van arrived. Selvig, Darcy, Lady Sif, and the Warriors Three jumped out.

Thor called Heimdall's name a third time. "Heimdall, we need you now!"

"He does not answer," Fandral said.

"Then we cannot return to Asgard," Hogun said.

In Asgard, Loki stood at the machine that opened the Bifrost. He used Gungnir to open it, and Laufey and his Frost Giants appeared.

"Welcome to Asgard," Loki said, and took them onto the Rainbow Bridge, past Heimdall, toward his father's palace.

Heimdall could hear Thor's voice. Asgard needed him, but he was still covered in ice. He was still Loki's prisoner!

Using all his power, he fought against the ice around him. Slowly it started to break, and the cold left his arms and legs. There was a Frost Giant standing next to him. Heimdall lifted his sword and cut through its body. Now he could help Thor.

He used his sword to open the Bifrost again.

On Earth, the sky filled with color and light. Everyone looked up. Above them, they saw the Bifrost!

"I must return to Asgard," Thor said to Jane. His eyes were full of love. "But I promise, I will return for you."

He kissed her hand.

She answered him with a kiss. And then it was time for Thor to go.

Jane watched sadly as he, Lady Sif, and the Warriors Three disappeared into the sky.

The Asgardians arrived quickly at the end of the Rainbow Bridge. "Take Volstagg to the hospital," Thor told the others. "I will go and find my brother."

He lifted Mjolnir, and the hammer carried him through the sky to the palace.

"I must return to Asgard," Thor said to Jane. His eyes were full of love. 'But I promise I will return for you."

The End of Loki?

Frigga sat by her husband's bedside. Suddenly, the door opened and a Frost Giant ran in. Frigga jumped up, lifted her sword, and cut it in two. Another Giant came in. It pushed her away, hard, and she fell to the ground.

Then Laufey came in. The Jotun king walked to Odin's bedside and looked at him. Slowly Odin opened his eye.

"It is said that during the Odinsleep you can see everything around you," Laufey said. "I hope that is true. Then you will know that I am your killer."

In his hand he held an ice knife. He lifted it up slowly …

Something hit Laufey from behind and he fell on the floor, badly hurt. He looked up at his attacker. It was Loki! Loki was pointing Odin's spear, Gungnir, at him. Strong, blue light poured from the spear into Laufey and his eyes closed.

"And Loki, the son of Odin, killed *you*," Loki said.

He shot at Laufey again with Gungnir.

The Jotun king didn't move again.

"Loki! You saved your father!" Frigga stood up and ran to Loki. She put her arms around him and started to cry.

"I promise, Mother, that the Jotuns will pay for this attack," Loki said.

"Loki!" called another voice from the door.

"Thor!" Frigga cried. She moved quickly away from Loki to her other son, and kissed him. "You are back in Asgard!"

Thor turned to Loki. "Why don't you tell Mother about the Destroyer?" he asked. "You sent him to kill my friends. And to kill *me*. Tell her!"

"What?!" Frigga said.

"The Destroyer was following Father's last order," Loki said.

"You are smart, brother," Thor said. "And you are a great story-teller. You always have been."

Loki smiled. "I am happy that you are here," he said. "But please excuse me. I am very busy. I have to destroy Jotunheim."

He lifted Gungnir and shot at Thor. The spear's power sent Thor flying through the wall. Frigga screamed and Loki ran out of Odin's bedroom.

Loki rode across the Rainbow Bridge to Heimdall's guard post and opened the Bifrost with the golden sword. Then he left it open.

Energy poured through the Bifrost toward Jotunheim.

Thor ran after his brother. He saw Loki in front of him and then he saw the Bifrost.

"Loki!" Thor shouted. "Close the Bifrost! Its energy will destroy Jotunheim and the Frost Giants, but innocent Jotuns will die, too."

He lifted Mjolnir. The hammer carried him up and into the guard post.

"You cannot stop it," Loki said. "The energy will build until Jotunheim is destroyed."

"Why are you doing this?" Thor shouted.

"I want to prove to Father that *I* am the good son!" Loki answered. "I saved his life. I will destroy the Jotuns and save Asgard! And when Father dies, I will be a good king!"

"You cannot kill every Jotun!"

"Why not?" Loki asked. "Why do you suddenly love the Jotuns? You *wanted* war with Jotunheim. You wanted to kill every Frost Giant with your own hands."

"I have changed," Thor said simply.

Loki laughed. "*I* have changed, too," he said. He hit Thor across the face with Gungnir. "Fight me," he ordered.

"I will not fight you, brother."

"I am not your brother!" Loki shouted.

"Loki, this is crazy," Thor said.

"Is it? What happened to you on Earth? Why are you now so soft?" Then Loki laughed. "Ah. It was that woman. Well, maybe, when we have finished here, I shall visit her."

Now Thor was, as Loki hoped, very angry. He held Mjolnir in front of him, and fought.

Loki hit Thor with Gungnir and Thor hit him back with Mjolnir. As they fought, they moved out of the guard post and back along the Rainbow Bridge. Energy was still pouring from the Bifrost into Jotunheim.

Suddenly, Loki fell over the side of the bridge!

"Brother, please! Help me!" he cried out.

Thor reached out his hand to help his brother … But then, with one of his mind tricks, Loki appeared behind him.

Loki hit Thor hard and Thor almost fell off the Rainbow Bridge. He turned. There were twenty Lokis around him, all laughing. Loki was playing more tricks with his brother's mind.

"Enough!" Thor cried.

He lifted Mjolnir and brought down lightning from the sky. It knocked down all the other Lokis. Now only the real Loki was standing, and Thor hit him hard with his hammer. When Loki fell onto the bridge, Thor put Mjolnir on his brother's chest. Loki could not move or escape from under it.

"Look at you!" Loki shouted from under Mjolnir. "Can you hear me, brother? You are so strong. Ha! You can do nothing to stop my plan!"

But Loki was wrong. Thor reached out his hand and called for Mjolnir. He lifted the hammer to the sky, then brought it down hard, again and again, onto the Rainbow Bridge.

Up in his room in the palace, Odin opened his eye. The Odinsleep was at an end and he was awake.

Loki jumped to his feet. "Destroy the bridge and you will not see that woman again!" he screamed.

Thor didn't look at him. He lifted Mjolnir higher.

"Forgive me, Jane," he said.

He brought the hammer down again. Most of the Rainbow Bridge broke into millions of pieces, the guard post fell, and the Bifrost was destroyed with it. Its energy stopped filling Jotunheim.

Only a small piece of the bridge was still standing. Thor and Loki fell back, over the side of it. Thor held onto it with one hand and held Gungnir in the other. Loki, below him, had one hand on the other end of the spear. They hung there, unable to move.

Thor tried to hold onto Gungnir, but the spear was falling from his hand. Then a strong hand reached down and took his arm. He looked up. It was Odin! After the Odinsleep, his father looked younger and stronger.

"I wanted to make you proud, Father!" Loki shouted. "To succeed for *you*! For all of us! For *you*!"

"No, Loki," Odin said sadly. "You opened Asgard to its enemies. You almost destroyed another realm and you almost killed your brother."

Loki looked at his father's face. There was no forgiveness there.

Thor saw Loki decide. "No!" he shouted.

Loki took his hand off Gungnir and fell. He disappeared into the endless sky between the Nine Realms.

"No!" Odin said quietly.

Loki took his hand off Gungnir and fell.

Down on Earth, Jane, Selvig, and Darcy were still in the street, looking up at the sky. There were strange clouds, lightning, and thunder up there. Something terrible was happening.

"He's gone," Darcy said.

Jane started to cry, and then she slowly followed her friends back to the van.

It was time to go home.

Two days later, there was a great party in Asgard. Laufey was dead and Jotunheim was peaceful again. Odin was awake and Thor was home.

Everyone believed that Loki was dead. Frigga was standing sadly alone, in a quiet corner of the room far from the main party.

Around the table, the Warriors Three were telling stories about their adventures on Earth. Thor smiled at them, but he too looked sad. He quietly left the table and walked out of the room.

Lady Sif watched him. She stood up and went to the queen. Frigga was standing next to a window now.

"My Queen," Lady Sif said. "I am so sorry about Loki."

"I am, too," Frigga said.

She was watching her husband and Thor. They were on the roof of the palace, looking out over Asgard.

"How is Thor?" Frigga asked.

"He misses his brother ... and he misses her. The woman," Lady Sif said.

"Yes," Frigga agreed. "We have all lost things that we love because of Loki."

Thor and his father looked down over Asgard.

"You will be a wise king," Odin said.

"There will never be a wiser king than you," Thor said. "Or a better father. I have a lot to learn. I know that now. One day, maybe you will be proud of me."

Odin put a hand on Thor's shoulder. "I am already proud of you."

He left Thor and returned to his wife. Thor walked out onto the broken end of the Rainbow Bridge. Heimdall was standing there, looking out at the stars.

"Earth is lost to us," Thor said. "The Bifrost is destroyed, so we cannot go there again."

"No," Heimdall said. "But there is always hope."

"Can you see her?" Thor asked.

"Yes."

Heimdall looked down at Jane, Selvig, and Darcy in their office. They were busy. There was a lot of work to do. There was a lot of sky to map. There were a lot of stars to look at.

"How is she?" Thor asked.

"She searches for you," Heimdall answered slowly.

Thor smiled. Yes, there was always hope.

Thor walked out onto the broken end of the Rainbow Bridge. Heimdall was standing there, looking out at the stars.

Activities

Chapter 1

Before you read

1 Look at the Word List at the back of the book. Check the meaning of new words in your dictionary. Then answer these questions.

   a Guns and knives are *weapons*. What other weapons are listed there?

   b What are the colors of the *rainbow*?

   c Which comes first, *thunder* or *lightning*?

   d Name three *objects* that you can see in front of you.

   e Name three things in your home that use *energy*.

2 Look at the Who's Who? pages at the front of the book. Then choose the right word to complete each sentence.

friend   *wife*   *brothers*   *assistant*   *son*   *enemy*

   a Loki and Thor are … .

   b Frigga is Odin's … .

   c Darcy is Jane's … .

   d Laufey is Odin's … .

   e Thor is Odin's … .

   f Dr. Erik Selvig is a … of Jane's father.

3 Now read the Introduction.

   a Name three of the Nine Realms of Yggdrasil.

   b Who must learn to be wise in this story?

   c Where must he learn this?

While you read

4 Write the speaker's name.

   a "What exactly are we looking for?" …………………………

   b "I'm not dying to pass my college course." …………………………

c "Where did he come from?" ....

d "A new day has come for a new king." ....

e "This is an act of war!" ....

After you read

5 **Work with another student. Have this conversation.**

Student A: You are Thor. You want to go to Jotunheim and fight the Frost Giants. Explain your reasons to Odin.

Student B: You are Odin. You do not want a fight between Asgard and Jotunheim. Explain your reasons to Thor.

6 **Think about your conversation in Activity 5. Who do *you* agree with—Thor or Odin?**

Chapter 2

Before you read

7 **Discuss these questions. What do you think?**

a What will Thor do next? Will he stay in Asgard or go to Jotunheim? Why?

b Who is the strange man on the ground near Puente Antiguo? Why is he there? What will happen to him next?

While you read

8 **Complete each sentence from the story with the right word.**

traitor	*sun*	*boy*	*destroy*	*lesson*
needs	*laws*	*actions*	*tricks*	*hospital*

a "We must teach them a ...."

b "Thor, you must not break the .... of Asgard."

c "Do you think you can use your .... on me?"

d "Which .... let the Jotuns in?"

e "If it stays open, it will .... Jotunheim."

f "You are a .... trying to be a man."

g "These are the .... of a boy."

h "Learn to put other people's _____ before your own."
i "O.K. We'll *all* go to the _____ ."
j "Blue sky, one _____ . Oh, no!"

After you read

9 Answer these questions in your own words. Give reasons for your answers.

   a What have you learned about Thor? What do you like or dislike about him? What is good or bad about him?
   b What have you learned about Loki? Do you think he is a good or a bad brother? Is he a friend or an enemy of Asgard?

Chapter 3

Before you read

10 Discuss these questions.

   a What happened when the Frost Giant touched Loki's arm? Why was he surprised? What is Loki going to learn about himself?
   b Thor is now on Earth with Jane and her friends. Does he have any power? What has happened to Mjolnir? What can Thor do next?

While you read

11 Complete each sentence with words on the right.

a The pictures from the storm	his hands turn blue.
b Thor wants more coffee	Loki becomes king.
c If Jane takes Thor to Mjolnir,	Odin took Loki.
d When Loki touches the casket,	talk to Frigga.
e After the war in Jotunheim,	show Thor's arrival.
f When the Odinsleep begins,	he will tell her his story.
g Loki refuses	so he breaks the cup.
h The warriors can't	to bring Thor home.

After you read

12 Work with another student. Have this conversation.

Student A: You are Thor. Everything on Earth is strange to you. Look around you. Ask Jane Foster questions about life on Earth. What do people eat? How do they travel? Then answer Jane's questions.
Student B: You are Jane Foster. Answer Thor's questions. Describe how people on Earth live. Then ask Thor questions about life on Asgard.

Chapter 4

Before you read

13 Answer these questions using the words below.

Loki   Thor   Selvig   Jane Foster   government agents
a government agent
Who will:
a steal Jane's work?
b take Thor to find Mjolnir?
c fight the government agents?
d help to save Thor?
e ask Thor a lot of questions?
f bring news about Asgard to Thor?

While you read

14 Are these sentences right (✓) or wrong (✗)?

a Agent Coulson takes Jane's van.
b Thor tells Jane about the Bifrost.
c Thor lifts Mjolnir out of the ground.
d Agent Coulson sends a gunman to watch Thor.
e Loki lifts Mjolnir out of the ground.
f Selvig helps Thor to escape from S.H.I.E.L.D.
g Thor takes Jane's notebook from S.H.I.E.L.D.
h Agent Coulson thinks that Thor is Dr. Donald Blake.

After you read

15 **Answer these questions in your own words.**

    a What is S.H.I.E.L.D.? Why is it in Puente Antiguo?
    b Who is Agent Coulson? Why doesn't he shoot Thor?
    c Why can't Thor lift Mjolnir out of the ground?
    d Why does Loki tell Thor that their father is dead?

16 **Discuss these questions with another student.**

    a What do you think about Loki? Why does he lie to Thor? Why is he so angry? Can you understand his actions?
    b Is Thor a different person now from the man at the beginning of the book? What lessons has he learned?

Chapter 5

Before you read

17 **Chapter 5 is called "Loki's Plan." What does Loki want now for himself and for Asgard? What do you think his plan is?**

While you read

18 **Circle the right answer.**

    a Loki leaves Thor and goes to … .
    Earth   Asgard   Jotunheim
    b Loki's father is … .
    Heimdall   Laufey   Odin
    c At the end of the Rainbow Bridge, Loki meets … .
    Heimdall   Laufey   Odin
    d Heimdall now works for … .
    Odin   Loki   Thor
    e Midgard is the Asgardian name for … .
    the Nine Realms   Earth   the World Tree
    f Loki sends the Destroyer to kill … .
    Lady Sif   Thor   the Warriors Three

After you read

19 Work with another student. Have this conversation.

Student A: You are Loki. Explain why you want to be king of Asgard. Describe your plans. What help do you ask for?
Student B: You are Laufey. Describe your feelings for Loki. Explain why you agree to his plans. What will you do next?

20 Explain Heimdall's actions in your own words. Why does he help the warriors? Why does he fight Loki?

Chapter 6

Before you read

21 In this chapter, Thor meets four friends and a terrible enemy. Who are they? What will happen when they all meet?

While you read

22 Put these in the correct order, 1–8.

a Thor offers his life to save the warriors.
b Thor learns that Odin is alive.
c The Destroyer arrives outside Puente Antiguo.
d The warriors arrive at Jane's office.
e The Destroyer hurts Lady Sif.
f The Destroyer walks away.
g The Destroyer hurts Volstagg.
h The Destroyer hurts Thor.

After you read

23 Answer these questions.

a Who gives the Destroyer orders?
b How does the Destroyer fight and kill people?
c Why does the Destroyer walk away from Thor and then come back?

24 You live in Puente Antiguo. You are in the café when Dr. Selvig runs in. He tells you to leave town. Describe what you can see in the street. What do you think is happening? Will you leave town or stay?

Chapter 7

Before you read

25 Is Thor dead? Will Lady Sif and the Warriors Three return to Asgard? Will Loki's plans succeed? What do you think will happen in this chapter?

While you read

26 Circle the right words.

a Outside the town, scientists are studying *Mjolnir / the Destroyer*.
b When Thor catches Mjolnir, *thunder / lightning* fills the sky.
c Thor wants to talk to his *father / brother* in Asgard.
d Agent Coulson says that S.H.I.E.L.D. *stole / borrowed* Jane's work.
e Thor asks Heimdall to open the *Bifrost / Rainbow Bridge*.
f He says that he *will / won't* be able to return to Earth.

After you read

27 Discuss these questions with another student.

a Jane says that S.H.I.E.L.D. *stole* her work. Agent Coulson says that his agents *borrowed* her work. What is the difference? Why do you think that Coulson agrees to return everything?
b S.H.I.E.L.D. agents protect the world from enemies, and they have a lot of power. What can happen to agencies or groups that have too much power? Give examples.

Chapter 8

Before you read

28 How do you think this story will end for

Thor? Loki? Odin? Jane Foster?

While you read

29 Use the word *before* or *after* in these sentences.

a .... Laufey comes into Odin's room, Frigga is knocked down.

b Laufey speaks to Odin .... Odin opens his eye.

c Thor comes into the room .... Loki kills Laufey.

d Jotunheim is saved .... the Rainbow Bridge is destroyed.

e Jane starts to cry .... she goes back to the van.

f Thor speaks to Heimdall .... Odin returns to the palace.

After you read

30 Describe the final battle between Thor and Loki. What happens to them in the end? What happens to the Rainbow Bridge, Heimdall's guard post, and the Bifrost?

Writing

31 You are Jane. Write a page of your notebook. Describe your first meetings with Thor. Where did he come from? What does he look like? How can he help your work? What more do you want to know?

32 You are Agent Coulson. You are going to question Thor after you find him near Mjolnir. Write a list of ten questions for him to answer.

33 You are a news reporter. Write a report of the fight in Puente Antiguo between Thor, his friends, and the Destroyer.

34 You are Erik Selvig. Write an email to your friend, Jane's father, after the fight in the street. Tell him what is happening in Puente Antiguo. Explain what worries you about Thor. What do you want Jane's father to do?

35 You are Loki. Write a letter to Odin, near the end of the story. Explain why you are angry with him and Thor. How do you feel about your family? Why did you let the Frost Giants into Asgard? What do you want to happen in the future?

36 You are Thor. Write a letter to Jane Foster—a letter that you cannot send. Tell her about your return to Asgard and your fight with Loki. Explain why you cannot go back to Earth. Tell her how you feel about her.

37 Write about this book for your local newspaper. Introduce the story, and the most interesting people in it. Will other readers enjoy it? Why (not)?

38 You are going to make another movie about Thor. Which people from this movie will be in it? Will Thor go to Earth again, or stay in Asgard? Who will he fight—and why? What will happen?

39 *Thor* is a science fiction story, about people from other worlds. Why are science fiction movies so popular? What other science fiction movies (or T.V. programs) have you enjoyed? Write about two of your favorites. Explain why you liked them.

40 Thor and Odin come from ancient northern European stories. Think of an old story from your own country that many people know. Write the story in your own words for other people to read.